THE SWINGING SWING AND OTHER SHORT STORIES

Medhini

i

Made   with   ♥   on   the   Notion   Press   Platform

www.notionpress.co

Dedicated to my husband, family, readers amd well wishers.

Contents

Foreword

If anyone tells you that life slows down after retirement and creativity, motivation and usefulness wither with retirement, don't believe them! No one belies this more than Medhini whose literary career burgeoned and blossomed post-retirement. Currently settled in Navi Mumbai, this bilingual writer spends her golden years crafting poems and short stories in both Malayalam and English.

Like so many of us who do not have the time to do things purely for pleasure during the busy years of our careers and working lives, Medhini too, took up literary work later in life to fulfil an inner urge' to jot on paper the feelings within her creative self.'

Medhini, now settled in Navi Mumbai, was born in the uniquely beautiful Malappuram district of Kerala, the home to four universities in the state, including the University of Calicut, and a hub of higher education in Kerala. Once a famous centre for Hindu – Vedic learning and Islamic philosophy, some of its culture is showcased in the writings of this worthy daughter from this intellectually fertile soil.

I have had the pleasure of working with Medhini (Anandavalli Chandran) in the early years of my career as a Secondary School English Teacher at Atomic Energy

Education Society, Mumbai. A graduate in Science and Education at that time, Medhini worked as a teacher in the Atomic Energy Schools in Mumbai, for almost thirty-three years.

A bilingual writer in both Malayalam and English, Medhini has published 3 Anthologies of Poetry and 3 collections of Short Stories in Malayalam. Her book of Poetry in Malayalam, published by Norton Press, is available at Amazon.In and flipkart.com. Medhini's two Poetry collections in English: 'Deafening Silence' (Collected Poems in English: Vol:1) and 'Undying Love' (Collection of Poems in English: Vol:2) have received accolades and awards from Critic Space Literary Journal, The Eternal Quest and Maharshi Vedvyas Book Contest 2023. These Poetry Collections are also available on Amazon.In and flipcart.com. Medhini's literary work has been featured in several national and international magazines, journals and newspapers. Her poem, 'Incredible India,' published in 'Canvas', the International e-magazine' (8 August 2024) conveys her patriotism and pride in the achievements of post independent India.

'The Swinging Swing and other Short Stories' is Medhini's first anthology and her foray into English Short Stories. As the representative story title suggests, the protagonist, Satyanath's mind swings to and fro like a swing, backwards and forwards in time, and draws the reader to the surprising twist at the end.

A common thread that binds all the stories together is the belief in humanity and positive relationships, whether they are the bonds between spouses, siblings, parents and children, friends or absolute strangers. Love in its 'many splendored colours' is dealt with, whether it is obsessive love, unselfish love, infatuation or loyalty and devotion that are components of love. 'Kindness Inspires Kindness' is a motivational story that emphasizes the value of treating people with kindness, empathy and respect. Some of the characters in the stories display courage in difficult situations and teach children to be brave, face their fears and stand up for what is right. And yet the characters who are imperfect and make mistakes are also dealt with empathy and understanding. After all, there are good people in Society too.

There are stories that deal with the spirit world as well as our relationship with the environment. So, this compilation of short stories has something suitable for every palate. With first-hand experience of the villages, customs and culture of 'God's Own Country', and her own distinctive style, Medhini has incorporated Malayalam words and phrases in some of her stories to showcase a way of life that many readers may or may not be familiar with. The short story, 'Bhutas (Ghosts) and Unclean Nocturnal Spirits' in particular, is set in rural Kerala of the 1950s and has a plethora of words taken from Malayalam but translated for those who are unfamiliar with the language.

The short story, 'Lazarus back from the Dead' has already been published by SHRIHIND PUBLICATIONS (Vividha samskaran-2) under the title, 'Dead Man Came Alive' and some short stories in this collection have been translated from their original Malayalam version.

In our cynical and selfish world today, Medhini's short stories appeal to all audiences, young and old, as the narration is simple and the themes are realistic and yet there is the touch of idealism that is so necessary to convey ideal truth in life and to also emphasize a person's spiritual fulfilment.

Mrs Dilys Lee

Master of Arts (English Literature) Master of Philosophy (ELT) B.Ed.

Senior Teacher English (Retd)

Education Department of Western Australia.

Preface

Welcome to "The Swinging Swing", a mesmerizing collection of short stories that promises to sweep you off your feet and transport you to a realm of profound wonder. Within these pages, the ingenious Medhini weaves a rich tapestry of human experiences, masterfully navigating the complexities of the human heart.

As you embark on this literary odyssey, you'll encounter a diverse cast of characters, each grappling with their unique struggles, triumphs, and transformative moments. With each story, Medhini skillfully orchestrates a symphony of emotions, deftly shifting between poignant introspection and humor, ensuring that every reader finds a reflection of themselves within these pages.

Medhini's writing is a triumph of subtlety and depth, as she distills the intricacies of human nature into narratives that are both relatable and profound. Her stories are threaded together by an unwavering empathy, compassion, and an unshakeable faith in humanity's capacity for resilience and redemption.

As you delve into the world of "The Swinging Swing", be prepared to oscillate between laughter and tears, reflection and revelation. Medhini's masterful storytelling will captivate your imagination, stir your soul, and linger in your thoughts long after you finish reading.

So, join Medhini on this unforgettable journey, and let the stories in "The Swinging Swing" enchant, inspire, and forever change the way you perceive the world and yourself.

Author name : medhini

Date : 27 february 2025

Author's Introduction

Born in Mangalam village in Tirur, Malappuram district, Kerala. Parents are late Smt. Kalyanikutty Amma and late Shri. Govindan Kutty Nair. Writes poems, stories and articles (in Malayalam and English). Poetry collections in Malayalam are "Mizhiyeerppam", "Orizha" and "Nina Padukal". Stories like "Kalikkoppukal,""Karutthirunda Meghangalude Rodanam" and children's stories "Balakathakalum, Kurunkathakalum" have been published in Malayalam. Her English works "Deafening Silence" (Collected Poems in English: vol:1) and "Undying Love" (Collection of Poems in English: vol:2) have received many awards. There are collective works with multiple authors' stories and poems in Malayalam and English. She has won the first prize in the Malayalam story writing competition of Pottekhat Memorial Committee (2024)

She is also the winner of the English Horror Story Competition, held by Femihive.

She has won the Jury Award for Malayalam Poetry conducted by Ee-malayalee Kavitha Malsaram 2024.

Medhini

Phone No: / Whatsapp No: +91 9920851697

Family :

Sons: 1. Bejoy Chandran

2. Benoy Chandran

Daughters- in- law: 1.Saroj Nair

2. Neha Sahay Benoy

Grand son: Shaurya

1. Her Whole World

Sajeeta, went against conventional norms with an interstate love marriage. At first, we, Sajeeta's parents, opposed her alliance with Ranjit. Our beautiful daughter was an air hostess with a reputed airline. Ranjit was an aeronautical engineer in the same company. They met each other about ten years ago and their relationship started as good friends. Gradually, they realised that their mutual trust was growing into attraction and something beyond friendship. On a Diwali day, when Ranjit met Sajeeta, he opened his heart to her and proposed marriage.

Though Sajeeta knew that one day she had to face this situation, she was not prepared to accept his proposal immediately. We, her parents, were not in favour of their marriage. However, Sajeeta insisted that Ranjit was a good natured, decent and dependable young man of good Punjabi parents. We belong to a middle-class Malayali family but we loved our daughter and finally agreed to their marriage. Within two months, they were joined in wedlock.

They did not plan to have a child for the first three years. But, another two more years passed and the couple began to get anxious as Sajeeta was not getting pregnant. They wanted to have a baby very badly and so they consulted a well-known gynecologist, on our advice. They were told that they didn't have a very serious problem but Sajeeta could conceive only through IVF or in vitro fertilization. For that they had to pay several visits to the doctor. The first two attempts were unsuccessful and Sajeeta failed to hide her frustration that she wasn't conceiving. We, too, were disappointed.

The gynecologist tried her best to give them hope and in the third attempt, Sajeeta became pregnant. All of us took great care to see that a healthy baby was born. Sajeeta avoided taking medicine for nausea and vomiting as she didn't want to jeopardize the little one growing within her. After nine months of pregnancy, on a Sunday morning her labour started she screamed with pain. We took her to the hospital and she was led to the labour room. Ranjit stood outside anxious and fearful.

Two hours passed. After performing a cesarean section, the doctor held up a healthy baby boy. For Sajeeta and the rest of us it was a great moment of exuberance and infinite joy. Sajeeta embraced the baby tenderly. After five days, when she was discharged from the hospital, she didn't want to part with her tiny one even for five minutes. Days and months passed. She was a busy mother now, running around, a slave to her little one's needs. She had become so possessive that she didn't allow Ranjit or me to feed the baby or give him a bath. An entirely new world had opened before this ecstatic mother.

The child thrived physically and emotionally but Sajeeta always clung to him. She had no time for anything else, other than feeding him, cleaning him, dressing him and playing with him. She even resigned her job to take care of him day and night. When her son started going to school, Sajeeta waited outside his classroom till he came out for her to take him home. She continued her overprotective, obsessive behaviour for a long time.

When Abhi, her son who was now twelve years old, fell sick and had to be hospitalized, Sajeeta used to sleep with him on the same hospital bed till the doctor strictly told her not to lie down with the young boy. Sajeeta wept bitterly but in accordance with the doctor's instruction, she spread a bedspread on the hospital floor and slept beside his bed – such was her devotion to her beloved son!

2. Unwavering Love

'My days are numbered. I won't be able to leave this hospital bed at all. Perhaps, I may end up h-e-r-e." Here Aruna's recurring fears and thoughts stopped abruptly. She saw her mother, Shobha, struggling hard to hide tears from her daughter. Aruna knew well that Shobha had brought her up with great care and showered love and blessings on her.

Shobha's thoughts went back twenty-four years. Aruna's actual parents, Nirmala and Madan had relocated to the city from Uttar Pradesh. They had four children - two sons and two daughters. Aruna was the youngest. They were staying two buildings away. Shobha, a South Indian, had two sons but no daughters.

One day, Shobha met Nirmala with her three-month-old daughter, Aruna. Shobha's love and interest in the child was immediate and Nirmala used to bring Aruna to her home daily and picked her up in the evening.

Later on, Aruna started staying in Shobha's house. She stayed in her own parents' house once a month. Shobha and her sons had great affection for her and Shobha's husband treated her as his favourite pet. The family spent many pleasant days with the little girl.

When Aruna was four years, Shobha got her admitted in kindergarten. She played the role of parent and teacher also at home. Every day, Shobha used to drop her off at school and bring her back home. She took pleasure in dressing Aruna and braiding hair neatly. Though Hindi was her mother tongue, Aruna learnt the language of her adopted family and spoke to them in fluent Malayalam. Shobha noticed Aruna's interest in dance and she admitted her in a dancing class where she learnt classical dance and was talented in Bharatnatyam.

Immediately after her Aarangethram programme, Aruna wanted to meet Shobha.But Shobha was in the crowd and she couldn't find her. This resulted in bitter weeping as she wanted to meet Shobha as soon as possible. Someone led the distraught girl to Shobha. Aruna began to kiss Shobha with such love in the midst of the crowd that people did not realise that she was actually Nirmala's daughter. How could Shobha ever forget that dear girl?

Aruna was a bright student, but still Shobha put her in a coaching class and she got ninety percent marks in the tenth exam. After she passed her Junior College (12$^{th)}$, she decided to do B.Sc. Computer Science in a college, not very far from home. Since she had to travel to and fro by bus. Shobha used to get worried whenever she came home a bit late. One day, Aruna fell down from the bus while alighting and she was not able to move her right foot forward. She sat on the roadside but she didn't want to trouble Shobha as she was well aware of her emotional nature.

After half an hour or so, Aruna's friend, Anisha, informed Shobha about the accident. In a panic, Shobha got into an autorickshaw and rushed towards her. Shobha was in tears but Aruna consoled her saying that nothing serious had happened to her but Shobha took her to the hospital, as quickly as she could. Shobha was so alarmed that she couldn't say anything to the doctor. She turned pale and fainted.

When Shobha regained consciousness, she saw Aruna's smiling face and she kept stroking Shobha with love in her eyes. The doctor told Shobha that he was more worried about the mother than the daughter. Aruna was discharged after a week without major complaints.

Aruna graduated in flying colours and joined MCA. In the midst of happy celebrations there was also grief as Shobha's husband expired during that time due to kidney failure. Aruna covered her face and cried very bitterly. She didn't eat anything for three days. In the midst of her own grief, Shobha struggled hard to comfort Aruna. After MCA, she got a good job in an IT firm.

One day Aruna came home with Ashok, her colleague, who was a Malayalee. Shobha's younger son, Anish, was at home and he approved of Ashok from the first meeting. Ashok and Anish became good friends but Ashok was still to meet Bipin, Shobhas's elder son, who was in London with his wife and daughter. After a year of courtship, Ashok asked for Aruna's hand for marriage. Shobha informed Aruna's birth parents, Nirmala and Madan about it and they gave the green signal to proceed.

Aruna and Ashok celebrated their first wedding anniversary just two months ago. But their happiness was short lived as Aruna had to be hospitalized due to a terrible pain in her abdomen. The doctor said that her kidneys were damaged and she would require a kidney transplant soon.

Shobha could not bear to look at the worried face of her adopted daughter. She was so young and sensitive and she was dealing with a great deal of pain. "Oh! God! Save her. God will hear my prayers. I am sure." Shobha could hardly think further as the doctor called her to the consultant room.

Before the doctor could say anything, Shobha asked him whether she could donate her kidney for Aruna's kidney transplant. Shobha went through all the required tests and had to undergo a thorough examination before the doctor informed that her kidney was a suitable match for Aruna. Shobha's joy knew no bounds but she didn't tell Aruna about it, fearing her reaction.

Today is Sunday, a holiday for most of the people, but it was the day of Aruna's kidney transplant. She was administered anesthesia while her family waited anxiously outside. The hours passed slowly. After what seemed like ages, the doctor came out, congratulated Ashok and told him about Aruna's successful kidney transplant operation. When Aruna regained consciousness after her surgery, the doctor told her that it was Shobha who had given her a new life. Aruna cried in gratitude.

'Though we are not bound by an umbilical cord, Aruna is my beloved daughter after all,' Shobha whispered to herself.

3. Lazarus back from the Dead

My husband was working in a private company. Then he switched onto the metallurgical division in another concern. He started travelling by local train to his work spot. Slowly he began to show signs of asthma and breathing difficulties. Once every month he was affected by this ailment. He was administered antibiotic medicines and given cough syrups. He was also advised by doctors to use Albuterol and Rescue inhalers during acute asthma. His health deteriorated due to frequent chest congestion and breathing trouble.

He had to be admitted to the hospital at least once every two months. Though he started using Ayurvedic and Homeopathy medicines, he couldn't find relief. Once, he got a high fever with acute breathing difficulty. He was hospitalized and had to undergo intense treatment. He lost appetite too. Finally, he succumbed to his illness after struggling for two weeks.

My physical condition became worse. I started losing weight and I was finding it difficult to sleep. I was getting choked up when I tried to speak to anyone. No words from relatives, friends and elders gave me solace. I lost interest in everything. No television shows, films, outings and visiting restaurants caught my attention.

My husband's body had been kept in the mortuary for one day and the next morning it was taken to the crematorium. Our children were beside him and performed the last rites. I saw neither the cremation hall nor the cremation. When we came home it was past two in the afternoon. Some of our relatives and friends cooked lunch and sent it to us. We couldn't sleep the previous night and had no food till then. Hence, we had some food and slept till six in the evening. I was only half asleep at that time. Old memories began streaming into the mind causing intense pain. Somehow, I couldn't believe that my beloved husband was no longer alive. My grief was intense and I did not know how to deal with it. This state continued for about six months.

When he was alive, my thoughts were not woven around him. We used to talk to each other and when angry, silence prevailed between us. Just three months after our marriage, we planned to go to a shopping town to buy some household items. He had told me that he would be waiting down, near the opposite building, pointing his finger towards the exact location. I agreed. When I went there, he was not to be seen. I was nonplussed. I got a bit worried too. Then I caught sight of him coming towards me from down the road. He smiled at me as if he had tricked me. I turned my face away from him as I was boiling with anger. When he called me to walk with him, I just followed him without breaking the ice. Now, this thought fills me with remorse and makes me gloomy, melancholic and depressed.

We had very few occasions to be away from each other. Once he went to his hometown for two weeks, but he came back only after twenty days. As soon as he entered our home, he embraced me. But I pushed his hands away and ran to the kitchen. He had felt very bad. I told him that I didn't feel hungry and both of us skipped lunch that day. In the evening, he bought a big red rose and placed it artistically in a flower vase on the table before me. I had never dreamt that he was romantic too. I brought him a glass of hot tea and some homemade sweets on a plate. He patted me on my back and we smiled and shared the tea and the sweets.

I took refuge in religion and began to pray a lot and visit nearby temples. Sometimes, I just sat near the window looking outside hoping for him to come home, in vain. In the middle of the day on the eleventh of June, I went into a trance. I felt that an unknown power was engulfing me. A familiar hand touched me on my back and I turned around. To my dismay, I couldn't see anyone around. Then I saw my husband standing in front of me. He lifted my chin with his right hand. I got a bit confused, wondering whether it was real or a dream. I stretched my hand to touch him so that I could make sure that I wasn't hallucinating. I was startled when I touched his face and arms. When he began to talk, words came out from his mouth in a whisper.

I began to pelt him with questions like ..."Where were you, all these years? Why did you go away, leaving me here? If you had thought of me, you would have come back soon. You didn't do it. Why? " Slowly he said. " I was not well, you know. I wanted a change of atmosphere. I am now in a better place – across the bridge where there's no more sorrow and pain, where the sun shines and you will never be unhappy again."

He had turned into my spiritual guide. He was always a very knowledgeable person and he now gave discourses on the Mahabharata, Bhagavad-Gita, Ramayana, and Upanishads for an hour each in the morning and evening. He chanted devotional songs beautifully. He narrated bible stories, fables, stories from the Panchatantra and teachings from the Quran. We walked around the Ashram, looking at the trees, shrubs and herbs and listening to the music of the birds in the early morning hours. When the sun was about to rise, the doctor and the inmates of the ashram walked towards the stream to have a bath, and enjoy the crimson of the rising sun reflecting in the water. I used to enjoy those things and it has brought me peace and acceptance and made me forget everything else.

4. Kindness inspires Kindness

Once Amina was travelling to the city by bus. The bus was not overcrowded and the conductor was doing his duty- issuing tickets and taking money back from the passengers. When the conductor asked a middle-aged man for the fare, he took out a few rupee notes from his wallet. While giving a few rupees to the conductor, three, two-hundred-rupee notes from his hand flew away, outside. Since he was busy keeping the notes back in his wallet, he didn't know about it immediately. When he realised it, the bus had moved forward a little. What was amusing to the passengers was that he didn't bother to alert the conductor or driver about it. When a few people remarked on it, he said, "I only wish that my two-hundred-rupee notes may reach the hands of a deserving poor man." Though he wasn't rich, he didn't bemoan the loss of his money. Amina really appreciated his concern and wishful thinking and said to herself, "We cannot find many people like him in our country today."

On another occasion, during a train journey, Amina witnessed a strange incident. She remembered that it was lunch time. The train stopped at the railway station. And many passengers had a hearty meal. Some people threw the leftover food on the railway track. Four or five poor children were pushing and running to grab the leftover food. A lady passenger, in her sixties, who was watching this, immediately purchased a few packets of food and distributed it among those hungry, destitute children. The hunger- stricken children grabbed the meal and smiled at the lady though they didn't know how to say polished words like "Thank you very much, madam." Within minutes, they finished their meals and when the train started moving slowly, they waved their hands to the kind lady with happy smiles on their faces, though other passengers were taken aback, they appreciated the noble lady's kind and thoughtful and immensely generous gesture.

It was raining heavily and Amina was walking slowly on the left side of the road holding her umbrella open over her head. An autorickshaw with a young lady, moved slowly and stopped in front of her. The lady got out of the rickshaw and walked on the narrow path between the paddy field. She noticed an old lady with a young girl, completely wet under a small open umbrella. The young lady along with the old lady and the girl slowly moved towards the rickshaw. The young lady asked them, "Where do you want to go?" They said 'Kalppatthi village' pointing in that direction. Their place was rather far, yet the young lady told them, "Don't worry, I will drop you at your home, so please get inside the auto." All the three gently got into the rickshaw and the driver moved forward. Amina was moved by the young lady's generous little deed of kindness.

After a month, on a bright, sunny afternoon, a boy of ten years or so approached Amina while she was returning from the market. The boy moved along with her, dragging a wheel cart of plants and flower pots and asked her to buy two or three potted plants. She didn't want to buy it immediately as it was not a necessity for her at that point in time. Besides, she had left home without money as well. However, when she looked at the boy's hungry, pinched face, she asked him to follow her home. When they reached her home, she served him food. She also asked her father to spare her some money and bought three potted plants. "Do you go to school?" she asked him. "No, deedi, my father passed away when I just completed fourth standard, so I left school and took up this work. My mother goes to other people's homes as a domestic help."

Amina told him to come to her house the next day. Amina's father was the owner and manager of a school and he had agreed to admit him in the fifth class after Ameena persuaded him.

In the evenings, the boy still engages himself in selling potted plants. Ameena, inspired by the kindness of people around her, also did a good deed. 'When you are kind to others, it not only changes you, it changes the world.' (Harold Kushner)

5. Rijesh's musings on Vimi the Peahen, loss of habitat and Zoos as Sanctuaries

A little away from the town there is a small jungle. It cannot be called a jungle but a small green area thickly crowded with trees. There are no wild animals like wolves, tigers and not even monkeys. The chirping and fluttering of a few small birds among the trees bring joy to the residents of the nearby area. The screaming noise of peacocks and peahens, sitting on the boughs, fill the air with sound and a feeling of awe at its majesty. Occasionally they come down and Rijesh's mother gives them grains, grams, tomatoes, etc, on large plates and Rijesh enjoys watching them eat.

There was a vast green area. It was a haven for beautiful birds. When people wanted more land for constructing houses, they formed a society and hacked the trees from a large portion of the area. They divided the land into small plots, built small terrace bungalows and allotted them to many people on payment. So, the beautiful birds including some peahens and peacocks flew away and settled in the nearby green haven. Rijesh heard this story from his parents as he couldn't remember all these things, and he was too small when it all happened. He felt very sad thinking of the plight of the small animals and birds.

Once, Rijesh saw a common hen like a bird but much bigger than a hen. He saw its head looked like a peacock. So, he asked his mother about it and came to know that it was a 'she' peacock or peahen. He had seen a peahen sometimes in the courtyard of the house. He didn't see the peahen for more than a month. He waited for some more days to see Vimi, that was the name he called her. Then, one day, he saw Vimi with two young ones in the courtyard. He felt happy and enjoyed seeing the young chicks peck at cabbage leaves. They looked very cute and beautiful.

Rijesh wondered, "Where do these pea-chicks come from?" His mom cleared his doubt saying that they were Vimi peahen's chicks. They have hatched from the peahen's eggs. "Oh! super!" he shouted. Rijesh admired the peahen more now.

Every day the two peachicks come near the bungalow with Vimi, the peahen. They eat cabbage and spinach leaves which are cut and given by Rijesh's mother. When Rijesh wanted to know why do the pea- chicks eat vegetable leaves, his mom made him understand that they can be easily eaten and they also contain proteins and minerals for their growth. He is thrilled when the peachicks start flying when they are about three months old. He saw them eating lizards, insects, spiders and worms. Rijesh does see them mostly on grassy areas nowadays, where they can spread and flutter their wings on a larger area. He takes care to watch their activities while standing a little away from them. He doesn't want them to fly far away from him.

Rijesh was curious to know where the peahens normally lived and laid eggs. His father told him that the peahen scrapes or scratches the ground with sticks to make a shallow hole there and covers it with layers of leaves and sticks. Peacocks and peahens stay there together. The peahen lays three, six or twelve eggs and sits over them for about a month or so. Only the peahen makes a nest and rears the peachicks. Though peacocks are very beautiful and attractive, they don't scratch the ground to make holes to stay and they don't take part in raising the peachicks. Sometimes the peahen makes a nest on trees, when predators are around.

Rijesh exclaimed, "My Vimi peahen is really a wonderfully hard worker and loves peachicks and peacocks very much." His parents felt very happy at his remark.

Five months have passed and the sixth month is starting now. The peachicks have grown and one of them resembles a young peacock with beautiful plumes. The other peachick looks like a peahen. Now they eat grams and fruits too. One day, Rijesh saw Vimi, the peahen pecking a long creature and sharing it with the peachicks. When he went a little nearer, he realized that it was a snake. When he watched the peachicks eat the pieces of snake he got frightened and ran home. After a month, he saw the peachicks roaming, searching for food, flying and spreading their plumes on their own, without Vimi, the peahen, nearby.

Days passed by. Rijesh saw some people start cutting the trees in the green area, near his house. He felt very sad as the green area was always filled with the chirping and shrieks of the birds while they were flying in search of shelter nearby. He couldn't see Vimi, the peahen and the lovely peachicks thereafter.

Instead, he saw a few workers building new concrete structures, maybe to make more houses in the near future.

Rijesh became very gloomy and upset. His parents could feel his disquiet and unhappiness and hence they thought of a plan. They told him that they could go to a far place for a change. Rijesh felt happy and welcomed the idea. The next Sunday, they started a train journey to visit a zoo. They reached the railway station after three hours. Then they went to a restaurant and had tea and snacks. Rijesh was very happy when he was served with vada and ice cream. After tea, they went straight to the zoo. Rijesh's father paid the entrance fee at the entrance counter and took the entry pass.

First, they saw rabbits and hares eating carrots. Rijesh noticed that the rabbits were white in colour whereas the hares were slightly brownish. Then they went to the monkeys' section. He was stunned to see the different kinds of monkeys and chimpanzees eating bananas and other fruits. The next area had crocodiles in shallow water. He watched snakes eating frogs. He found small and big snakes there. He was delighted at the sight of iron fencing and barricades around the dwellings of the animals. They saw deer too.

Rijesh saw fierce lions along with another kind of animal. When Rijesh asked questions about it, his mom explained to him that the huge one with a mane was a lion and the long animal without a mane was a lioness. His mother took him to the next cage where the lioness played with her cubs. Similarly, when he saw the tiger, he pointed out the difference. Rijesh's dad explained to him that the orange-coloured animal with slightly curved black lines was a tiger and the one without black lines was a tigress. When Rijesh wanted to know what the young ones were called, his dad told him that the young ones of both the lioness and the tigress were called cubs.

Rijesh found parrots of different colours and peahens. He was happy to see the peahens and peachicks as he missed Vimi, the peahen and her peachicks. Rijesh was reluctant to leave the zoo with his parents in the evening. He realised that the zoo was a safe haven for the animals and he hoped that one day, he could become an environmentalist or zoologist and help to save the planet.

6. Pegasus and Pedavire

Pushkar and Kishore were good friends. Their houses were not very far away. Pushkar was a grocery shop owner; Kishore, younger to Pushkar by four years, ran a sweet-shop. Pushkar married Chitthira, a young woman from his village. Both of them got good profit from their business and provided for their families.

Three years after Pushkar's marriage, he made arrangements to get Kishore married to Athreya, an attractive woman from a nearby town, the only child of her parents. Since Pushkar and Kishore had to run their businesses almost all days, except for a few public holidays, they were unable to take their wives for fun trips to the cinema or for any other outings. Chithira carried on with her household work without grumbling or showing any resentment or irritability to her husband, but Athreya, the new bride, was less tolerant with the new situation and found it very difficult to adjust. Initially, she went to her parents' house and spent a few days there. Two years passed like this. Then Pushkar suggested a solution to this. He advised Kishore to start his sweetshop near his grocery shop. Kishore consulted Athreya and agreed to it. When Kishore took leave to go out with his family, Pushkar looked after the business in both the shops. Kishore did the same when Pushkar went out with his wife, Chitthira, and his family. So, both the families led a harmonious life, balancing both work and entertainment.

Many years passed by. Pushkar wanted to buy a horse, as it was his favourite animal right from his early childhood. Pushkar discussed the matter with Kishore and one fine morning, they bought a healthy, black, shiny foal. Pushkar tied the young horse in a shelter attached to his house. The foal was fed with cooked horse gram and oats.

Athreya called the foal Pegasus and everyone followed her and called the foal by that name. Pushkar, Chitthira, Kishore and Athreya always hung around Pegasus, to feed him and give him a bath. Within a few months, Pegasus grew into a medium sized horse. Pushkar kept Robin, a jockey, to train Pegasus, ride him and take care of him so that he could participate in horse races.

After months of training, Pushkar allowed jockey Robin to take Pegasus for a race. Both Pushkar and Kishore took their families to watch the race. Kishore bought a few tickets to bet on the race. While Pegasus was running, Pushkar stood motionless, holding his breath in nervous anticipation. There was great excitement and everyone applauded when jockey Robin was literally flying on Pegasus. Pegasus won the race after racing two thousand four hundred metres. The two families reached home by eight in the night. A splendid dinner was arranged at Pushkar's house for both the families. After the meal, a chat session followed as it was a great day for them.

The next day, Kishore expressed his desire to buy a horse for himself. That evening, they bought a stoutly built, brown horse and brought him to Kishore's house. Pushkar's family was there. They put the horse inside the shed and fed him cooked horse gram. Everybody had dinner at Kishore's house. They shared sweets happily and Chitthira suggested the name Pedavire for the horse. All of them liked the name. When Kishore went to the shop, Athreya took care of Pedavire. Pushkar delivered oats and grams in Kishore's house free of cost. Kishore exchanged sweets with Pushkar's family. Athreya had learned to make many sweets and delicacies from Chitthira.

When an auspicious day arrived, Pegasus and Pedavire were taken to the racecourse by Pushkar, Kishore and jockey Robin. Pedavire was trained for this auspicious day by Robin.

Pushkar took control of Pegasus while Robin took care of Pedavire. Both the families of Pushkar and Kishore were seated at the boundary of the field to witness that interesting race. Both Pegasus and Pedavire raced well almost to the end. Finally, Kishore's horse finished two thousand five hundred metres to reach the first position. Both the families went home happily and had meals by nine that night.

Kishore appointed another jockey, Sathish, to train Pedavire to participate in another horse race. Everything was going smoothly with Pushkar's family and Pegasus and Kishore's family and Pedavire. Another chance to participate in the horse race knocked on their doors.

Both Pegasus and Pedavire were well-prepared under the guidance of jockey Robin and jockey Sathish. Both the families eagerly watched the race and cheered wildly and clapped boisterously for black Pegasus and brown Pedavire. Ultimately, Pegasus won the race. Everyone enjoyed the races and had an enjoyable time.

Kishore and Athreya seriously thought about a change of routine in their life. They went on a tour to Kashmir for a week, leaving Pedavire in the care of Pushkar and Chitthira. Athreya and Kishore enjoyed the beautiful floating Shikaras with flower sellers on the Dal Lake and stayed in a houseboat for two days. When they returned, they shared their pleasant experiences with Pushkar and his family.

In the middle of May, both Pegasus and Pedavire were taken to the race course again. Pegasus completed two thousand five hundred meters and was the winning horse in first position. Pedavire was the first runner-up. Both Pushkar and Kishore received a huge sum of money. After the race, the families of Pushkar and Kishore went to watch a movie that they enjoyed thoroughly.

In the next three races, which were held in October and November, Pedavire lost the race and Kishore ran out of money. At the same time, Pegasus raced to success in all these races and Pushkar gained a lot of money. Kishore was disheartened and lost interest in everything.

Quite a few people told Kishore, secretly, that Pushkar had connected Pegasus spy- ware to his mobile phone. Was this true or false? And did it destroy a friendship and perfect relationship?

7. Bhutas (Ghosts) and unclean Nocturnal Spirits

My memory goes many years back. It was the last Friday of October. My mother told me the other day that certain things are badly haunting us. My father fell down last October and since then he is not able to walk and is bedridden. She said we have to do something about it. I didn't understand anything then. We, the four siblings, returned home from the primary school at 4.30p.m. We saw three women workers busy grinding rice into flour in a long wooden mortar (okhli) in the thatched roof shed. We looked at the women pounding the flour for some time and then ran to the kitchen for homemade snacks and coffee. After changing our school uniform, we returned to the palm frontroofed shed and were surprised to see green powder from the dry, green leaves, turmeric powder and black powder from the burnt paddy chaff, laid out on old newspapers. The women had been very busy. They explained how they had made different coloured powders for the ensuing function.

When it was around 7.00 pm the priest and his assistant arrived. There was a medium-sized jamun tree growing in the sandy soil, further far away from home. The priest's assistant removed the grass from a small space under the tree. Two irregular, uneven, grey rock pieces were arranged a little apart from each other. The rock piece on the left side represented Gulikan and the piece of rock on the right side was Parakkutty. (Both are evil spirits that cause trouble at home.) "Usually, people don't pray to them", said the manthravaadhi (priest, enchanter or sorcerer). We had never heard of these evil spirits before and so were curious.

The different coloured powders were brought there and the manthravaadhi made two rectangles, with white rice flour, a little away from each other. Inside each rectangle, he made twelve squares and filled them with different coloured powder like green, white, yellow and black. A lantern was lit and kept a little away from each rectangle. Each bronze vessel with a spout (kindi) filled with water was kept near each lantern. Two brass plates with flowers were kept on each side. Two bronze bowls of rice flakes were also placed in a row near two trees, a little away from the Gulikan and Parakkutty rock pieces. The sacrificial birds had their legs tied with a small, thin rope. We were paralyzed with fear when we heard the shrill noise coming from the basket.

The manthravaadhi sat on a flat wooden stool, supported by two small bars of wood that were fixed two inches from the ground (palaka). He sat in front of the two pieces of rock, and started chanting some sacred utterances (mantras) while offering the flowers. After a few minutes, his assistant told us to turn around with our backs to the rock pieces. Then, we heard some frightening shrieks. When we turned to face the rock pieces, we could see the severed heads and bodies of the two cocks on a coconut frond. We were stricken at the sight. The manthravaadhi's helper carried the heads and bodies of the cockerels to a far-off place, while the manthravaadhi and the rest of us went home. My mother and elder sister were busy cooking and so we started playing some indoor games.

After an hour, the manthravaadhi told us to accompany him to Gulikan and Parakkutty's ground. He told us to take the bronze bowls of rice flakes, brass plates with flowers and lanterns to keep at home. He took two banana leaves with food from the kitchen and walked towards the pooja (prayer) site. By that time his assistant and the elders of the family had reached near the jamun tree.

The manthravaadhi started chanting mantras, with the offerings on the banana leaves stretched in his hands towards the site of the rock pieces. We turned our backs from the pooja site for some time as we were instructed. When we turned around, the helper with the food offerings on the banana leaves was not there. Two bronze lamps with two small, white threads in each and submerged in oil, were brought to the pooja site. The priest kept the bronze lamps a little away. He lit each of them and chanted hymns. At his direction, we joined our palms and prayed. To be exact, the offerings to Gulikan and Parakkutty and the other rituals took place in 1955. Soon after that, all of us left for home with the lamps and bronze kindikal.

The manthravaadhi and his assistant washed their feet, hands and face and came to the entrance hall for dinner. Mother served them dinner and my elder sister served us dinner in the room next to the kitchen. We finished dinner within twenty minutes. After dinner, the priest and his assistant left. It was around 11. 30. p.m. and so we siblings went to the bedroom and made our beds to sleep. Our house was in a village and electricity didn't reach our homes in those days. So, mother lit a kerosene lamp and kept it in our room. When mother and our eldest sister had dinner, we were almost asleep. I had an uneasy feeling as I lay down in bed.

Soon my sisters and brother were in deep sleep. I too wanted to sleep and closed my eyes. I didn't know how much time had passed when I heard some eerie sounds. I strained my ears and I could hear shrieks outside. But I couldn't recognize whether it originated from animals or birds. It was coming closer and I felt that the shrieks were from the top of the coconut tree standing near the jamun tree. I could see two pitch dark figures climbing down the coconut tree till they reached the ground. Slowly, they started walking towards our house. "Oh, no, no" they were gliding towards our room. There was a tall, branching mango tree, near a coconut palm on the land behind our room.

The two fearsome figures stood there, leaning against the coconut palm. They were visible to me. One was short, fat and jet black with the body of a man. His eyes were large and round rays of fire came out of it. He shrieked, "I am Gulikan," and was silent afterwards. The other figure was tall and looked feminine and was fully green in colour. She cried bitterly and screamed, "I am Parakkutty." She had very long, thick, straight hair and sharp white teeth. Both of them stamped on the ground around the mango tree, sending out blood curdling screams. I put my fingers in my ears and closed my eyes tightly.

Both the evil spirits walked towards the window of our room and called my name, 'Lathe' in a soft voice. They asked me to come out to the courtyard. I didn't respond to that. Then they called my name, 'Lathe' many times in the affectionate tone of my elder sister and mother. A prolonged and profound silence ensued. Suddenly, I heard 'Manju, Manju' in a manly voice resembling my father's. My father is the only person who calls me Manju. So, I was about to get up and go towards him. My real name is Manju Latha. When I heard shrieks from somewhere, I thought it must be Gulikan. My body began to shiver with fear. I wanted to scream loudly, but my throat got choked and no sound would come out. I felt helpless and sought my mother.

I could see Gulikan's body completely wrapped in fire, while Parakkutty began spitting out fire. Petrified, I prayed to God for help. I really didn't know whether to run out of the room or to lie down with my eyes shut tightly. The fiends came very close to the window. Our window bars and doors were made of wood.

Two window bars and a window frame started burning. "Move away from the window. Please don't burn the window," I pleaded with them. I wanted to fetch some water from the kitchen to put out the fire, but I was not able to get up and move. After some time, when I had gained a little strength and courage, I ran to the kitchen and filled a small bucket with water. I picked it up and rushed to our room. I flung the water on the window bars from a distance and quenched the fire. Gulikan and Parakkutty shouted and screamed. I brought another bucket of water and kept it in a corner of the foyer. I saw the evil spirits standing still, a little away from our room window. It seemed to me they were scared of water. I quickly ran out of the house and stood near the jamun tree. The demons didn't approach me there.

When I looked back, I saw Gulikan and Parakkutty moving towards me. "Will I have to face the same ordeal again?" I wondered and thought of myself dying in that process.

Then I remembered that they were scared of water. So, I ran towards the small pond, located in the distance. Without thinking twice, I jumped into the pond. It was deep and I swam in the pond, paddling my hands and legs. I saw them coming towards me again, but they stood far away from the pond. In the firelight that came from their mouths, I saw a water snake raising its head in the water. I darted out of the water and ran full pelt. They couldn't run behind me so fast. Exhausted, I sat under a jackfruit tree. I started hyperventilating. Then I got a foul smell of burning corpses. I couldn't locate the source of the fetid smell. I felt like vomiting and got up and walked towards the thatched shed. I sat on the okhli for some time.

Our dog, Kaisar, was sleeping there in the north - south direction. When he saw me, he began to whimper, but when I massaged his back, he wagged his tail and walked around me. All of a sudden, Kaisar started whimpering and cowering, ears flat against his skull, his eyes wide and muscles tensed with his tail tucked between his legs. I found two dark figures moving around the jackfruit tree. After some time, they sat behind the tree. Kaisar stopped barking. The dark figures moved slowly in the north-west direction. Perhaps, Gulikan and Parakkutty had given up their chase. I hoped so. In the shed, there was a small compartment made of woody branches and planks. Our young, six-month old goat slept there at night. Out of curiosity, I looked around the goat shed and to my surprise, I found the goat sleeping without any hindrance or disturbance. All of a sudden, the thought came to my mind that the thatched shed was not safe for me or the goat or Kaisar. The green coconut fronds were split into two straight halves and the women workers were weaving them in a special way. These plaited coconut leaves are used for making the thatched roof and walls of the shed. Almost a year had passed since we built this shed. The thatched leaves of the shed are dry now and can catch fire easily. So, I left the shed (uralppura), walked towards the well and stood there.   There was no sign of Gulikan and Parakkutty. So, I breathed a sigh of relief.

After about fifteen minutes, I heard the now familiar shrieks and turned around but I couldn't see anyone. Then someone pushed me from behind. Though I was taken aback, I jumped with all my might and reached the courtyard on the opposite side of the well. It was a narrow escape as I could have fallen into the well. When I looked up, I just had a glance of Gulikan walking away. I was paralyzed with fear when I saw Gulikan and Parakkutty dragging my younger sister and coming forward. Suddenly, Gulikan grew into a gigantic figure. He tied my sister's legs with a red ribbon, lifted her body with his hands and threw her into the well. For a few seconds, I didn't know what to do to save her. I pulled the bucket with a rope tied on it from the kitchen and slowly lowered the bucket with the rope into the well.

"Mole, catch hold of the bucket and rope," I shouted. She did as I told her. Slowly I lifted the bucket with her and brought it to the courtyard. Gulikan and Parakkutty were not to be seen. I told my sister, Leela, to go and sit in a corner of the hall (poomukham) and she obediently followed my instructions.

As I was standing in the courtyard in front of the well, Gulikan and Parakkutty came on the other side of the well and started jumping and dancing with loud, bestial laughter, rejoicing at the thought that Leela must have drowned in the well. Gulikan's eyes were bulging out and his huge teeth projected out, while saliva dribbled down from his mouth. I started weeping. Then Parakkutty also followed Gulikan, sending out harsh shrieks. It was a terrible sight. They disappeared for a while and then Parakkutty appeared dragging my youngest sister, Neena. Neena was crying bitterly and struggling in Parakkutty's tight hold. Parakkutty was spitting out fire as well. I ran to the foyer, where I had stored a bucket of water and carried it near the well. Parakkutty was trying to spit out fire and burn Neena's left hand. I threw the water from the bucket into the demon's mouth and the fire was extinguished temporarily. I grabbed Neena's hand and ran. I then examined Neena's left hand. The skin was scalded and had turned reddish. I instructed Neena to apply saliva from her mouth on the inflamed area of her left hand. She did as I told her and it brought relief to her sore and stinging skin. I caught hold of her with my right hand and with the bucket in my left hand, ran towards the small pond near the jamun tree.

In fear, we watched Gulikan and Parakkutty running towards us with my younger brother in their clutches. Gulikan released his grip from my brother, but Parakkutty held onto my brother, Neelesh. Then Gulikan started throwing handfuls of sand onto Neelesh's body. Neelesh, in turn, began throwing sand into the eyes of the demons. All of us began to throw sand at them. I filled half the bucket with sand and threw it at them. They retreated and we walked towards our home.

When we entered the foyer, Leela was in the corner half asleep. I woke her up by banging loudly on the front door. Father opened the door and all four of us went inside. Father didn't question us. He must have thought that we were sleeping in the entrance room. We all clamoured to sleep in his room. He agreed. We brought our mattresses from the room in which we had been sleeping earlier. We were scared but we didn't say anything to our father. We tried our best to sleep. Meanwhile, my father started snoring. His snoring comforted us because we felt that our father would protect us from danger. We siblings huddled close to one another and tried to sleep. Half an hour later, I heard loud footsteps outside in the courtyard. Fear crept in once more and I felt a chill running down my spine.

Father woke up, took his walking stick and went to the attached washroom. As he was walking, we could hear footfalls in the courtyard. After sometime father returned to bed and we didn't hear the sound of footsteps in the courtyard after that. Though I tried, my sleep was interrupted due to fear and anxiety. After what seemed like ages, I could hear loud shrieks interspersed with howling sounds. A chill began to creep in my heart and my siblings were terrified. Father took a long iron rod from the corner of the room and pushed and pulled backwards and forwards the wooden window bars. Soon the shrieks and howling vanished. We felt happy and safe.

I heard a few knocks on the doors of the north side of the house. At least I thought so. When no one opened the door, I could hear loud banging sounds which soon led to thrashing. The dogs in the neighbourhood barked non-stop. I realised that Gulikan and Parakkutty had not left our house.

You could hear the cow and calf lowing, bellowing and bawling in the cow shed. Our dining room and the adjoining area is connected to the cowshed. After some time, the knocking, banging and thrashing of the door on the north side stopped. Our tharavad or ancestral home is a large one with two bedrooms, a middle room and two long halls, one on the north side (vadakkini) and the other on the south side (thekkini) on the ground floor. We have three upstairs rooms too, with a corridor but we usually do not sleep here. The stairs from this floor take us to another hall with a low roof (thattinpuram) where we play hide and seek. but we don't go there during the night. After our hair-raising experience with the evil spirits, we don't go there during the daytime either. I will never forget those ominous shrieks and screams and the ensuing nightmares that traumatized me for many years afterwards.

Glossary

Okli - Mortar

Uralppura - A small shed used for pounding paddy and grinding rice into flour Gulikan and Parakkutti – Spirits that cause trouble

Manthravadhi - Sorcerer or enchanter

Palaka- A small long and flat stool of 2 or 3 inches of height for sitting with legs crossed.

Kindi - A bronze lotta with a spout

8. The Swinging Swing

Only nine days left for the Lifetime Achievement Award to be bestowed on me, Sathyanath thought. He had butterflies in his stomach just thinking about the moment he would receive the prestigious award. So far five of his acclaimed novels - 'Dark Clouds,' 'Pouring Rain,' 'Distant Light,' 'Withered leaves and 'Deathbed' were published and a biography titled 'The Swinging Swing' was yet to be published.

"I don't deserve this. My younger sister is destined to remain in a dark room due to behavioural problems. She asks for food to be served to her. When she gets a pen and book, she scribbles something in the book day and night. 'Days, months and years passed. I used to go to her room to give her food and water and to keep a pen and book on the table.

The first published book was 'Dark Clouds.' What was the theme of that book? It was about a smart nine-year-old girl who was studying in school and attending 6th std classes regularly. One day, when the class was ongoing, she started rolling on the floor of the classroom, foaming from her mouth. Her classmates and teachers were terrified at the sight. Her body was tense and then it began to jerk rapidly. Her eyes kept moving from side to side; she was sweating, her skin was pale and her teeth were chattering. The class teacher brought a small steel spoon of water and inserted it in her mouth in between her teeth. Nobody knew what to do. After some time, she recovered and was sent home with the school peon.

After three days she returned to school like any normal child. She told the teacher that the doctor had diagnosed her problem as epilepsy. Slowly all the children in her school came to know about her seizure disorder and began to isolate her socially. They started spreading rumours about her medical condition and were fearful that it would spread to them too. Their parents decided that it was better for them to keep away from her. The little girl felt lonely and isolated in school. Thereafter, she refused to go to school. She could see light nowhere and saw only dark clouds in her life. Thus, the story ended.

The next book, 'Pouring Rain,' flashed in Satyanath's memory. A young lady was travelling by train in the rain. Suddenly there was a heavy downpour and the train came to a halt. The railway tracks were flooded. She looked around but only a young man and a young girl, (maybe his sister) were seated in the compartment. The train had halted a little away from the platform and an announcement over the loudspeaker stated that the train was not able to proceed further for a few hours.

"Let's get down here."

"No, it's night time."

"You come with me. My home is not very far away from here. Trust me, madam." The three of them struggled to get down and then walked about two kilometres to reach his home. The young man dropped her home the next morning. In this time, they exchanged addresses and interests and soon they became long lasting friends. "This novel too has reached an end," Sathyanath thought.

The book 'Distant Light 'was Satyanath's favourite. A childless couple had a desperate desire to have a baby of their own. Modern science, especially in the field of fertility, had not developed much at that time. A few well-wishers advised them to adopt an orphaned or abandoned baby. But was there any known person who would be ready to give away their own child? That was the main problem.

The couple waited for two more years to get a chance for adoption. Then they approached an orphanage and were able to legally adopt a five-month-old girl, without any obstacles in their way. The couple felt very happy bringing up the child. Her presence at home brought fulfillment and heavenly light in their home. The girl grew up and wanted to pursue higher education in Canada. Her adopted parents initially tried to persuade her to continue further education in India, but finally they succumbed to her wishes. While continuing her studies abroad, she kept contact with her parents frequently and their mutual love shone brightly in their hearts.

A young, intelligent and motivated scientist of biology was engaged in doing research and experiments in crossbreeding. He cross-fertilized different kinds of rose plants and produced white, orange, purple, brown, green and black hybrid roses from the rose plants. Next, he tried to get mutants by crossing and mutating jersey cattle and a common breed of cows. He failed in the first attempt but he continued his efforts. But all his attempts were unsuccessful and proved to be like withered leaves. He burnt all his research notes in disgust and despair. Sathyanath didn't read further about the novel, 'Withered Leaves.'

It was a full-scale war between Russia and Ukraine and many Ukrainians were killed defending their country in battle. A few Russians also lost their lives but the war continued. The novel, 'Deathbed' narrates the story of an old woman who was mortally wounded by a number of gunshots but she was still alive, writhing in pain. Her husband, her three children and her immediate neighbours were also killed in the skirmish. Her condition was pathetic and there was no one around to take care of her or move her to the hospital. Her deathbed was hard, barren ground filled with stones, and the debris from buildings. Sathyanath didn't want to think further – he terminated these unpleasant thoughts.

Sathyanath started asking himself feebly, "Where am I? How did I come here?" In the meantime, a young man came there, held his hand and checked his pulse. After that a lady drew some blood from the inside of his arm with a syringe and needle. Sathyanath asked the young man, "Who are you? What are you doing here?"

"I am a doctor. You are quite well, Sathyanath. You have been sleeping here for the past seven days. You must have consumed eight or ten sleeping tablets. You are the author of many books. You are well-known." The young doctor spoke at length. Sathyanath could vaguely remember what had happened.

"Yes, doctor. I must have swallowed a few sleeping tablets but I don't recall it exactly. I have not written the books."

He sprang up to his feet.

"It is my younger sister, Maidhili, who is the author of those books. I have only written the last two pages of the book. 'The Swinging Swing' is part of my revelation of an unpardonable action but that book isn't published yet. I believe I am guilty of passing off my sister's work as my own," Sathyanath sobbed in shame and despair.

9. Sharanalayam

Nivedita stood on the bank watching the water level of the important lake of the city rise in the rain. Suddenly she noticed a few small bubbles in the water, a little far from the shore and was surprised to see violet spots on an orange dress. "Maybe young. No time to think," Nivedita reflected. She jumped into the water and with all her strength, held the young girl with her right hand and paddling with her other hand and legs somehow brought her ashore. Holding her and shaking her, Nivedita asked, "How did you get into the water? Did you slip? Or did you try to swim?" The girl slowly opened her eyes, but she was not able to speak.

Pointing to the bag lying a little away, Nivedita asked the girl, "Does that bag belong to you, child?"

"Yes," she replied.

Relieved, Nivedita sighed and said, "You are able to speak. What's your name girl?"

She did not answer. Nivedita felt that she was a little older than she first thought.

"I am opening this bag."

Nivedita took a towel from the bag and gave it to her saying, "Wipe your hair thoroughly with this towel and come with Niveditha chechi."

Where to?"

"I will tell you later. Hold my hand and walk forward with me. You are very tired." Nivedita said this and walked forward holding her hand.

Nivedita flagged down an autorickshaw.

"Get in this auto. Be quick." Saying that, Nivedita also got in with her and told the driver where to stop. After ten minutes, Nivedita told the driver to stop at a gate. The driver stopped the auto and Nivedita got down holding her companion's hand. "We have to go to this house. Don't be scared." They both entered the house.

"Ammae, ammae, come here. Look who's here." Nivedita called out.

"Who is she, dear?" I don't understand."

"Ammae, didn't I tell you about visiting Powai Lake, this rainy season. That's where I went. It's good that I went there, Amma."

"And you both swam in it? You're all wet." Mother anxiously said.

"I'll tell you everything in detail. Excuse me. Ammae, go, pour some milk in a glass and give her some Horlicks," Nivedita said as she went upstairs.

The girl was drinking the Horlicks, when Nivedita came downstairs after changing her clothes. She brought clean, dry clothes for the girl who smiled gratefully at them.

The girl changed her clothes and came downstairs.

"Did you find time to eat, Achuthan Embranthiri? Go and have lunch. I will stay here till then."

When the manager said, "I have come here for lunch," Mother felt happy.

"Honey, Nive, call that girl too. All of us can eat together.

Everyone was about to eat, when Achuthan asked, "Is she your friend? "

Was she not a friend?

Now, she is my friend and a member of our family too, Eatta," Nivedita answered.

After lunch, Achuthan left.

After the meal Nivedita went upstairs with her new friend. They sat on a bed and started talking.

"You didn't even tell me your name, friend," Nivedita said with sisterly affection. "Chechi, mother and all of you can call me Janu from now on".

Nivedita agreed and realised that Janu has something important to say.

"Aren't you all Embranthiris?" (High Brahmin caste) I belong to a low caste - Thiyyatthi. So, it is not right for me to stay here with you. Please let me go. I will find a place for myself somewhere." She paused.

"Janu, we don't need any distinction between upper castes and lower castes. Aren't we all human beings?" You sleep well now." Nivedita very kindly patted Janu on the shoulder.

Two weeks passed. The following Wednesday, Achuthan Embranthiri was waiting at the bus stop to take his mother and Janu to the hospital as his mother was not feeling well. As the bus came roaring in, Janu darted in front of the bus. Achuthan Embranthiri quickly grabbed her left hand and dragged her to safety. He asked her angrily, "Janu, what are you doing? If you run like this, won't you fall under the bus? Nothing happened because I reacted quickly." Janu was repentant. Then she noticed that Achuthan's right elbow was bleeding. She bought Dettol and a band aid from the next stall, cleaned Achuthan's elbow and stuck the band aid on the graze.

Everyone came back from the hospital and Nivedita also came home after work. After drinking tea and chatting, Nivedita called Janu upstairs. "Janu, why did you behave so foolishly? Why did you jump in front of a moving bus? What would you have done if your arm and leg were broken or something worse had happened?"

"That's not it, chechi. What's the point of living like this?" Janu could not complete her sentence. Nivedita intervened. "Why are you so unhappy? Are you a college student? Are you afraid of failing your exams?"

"That's not the problem, chechi. I have written my final year B.Sc. exam. No fear of failure. "I can tell you, chechi, can't I?"

"You should," Nivedita replied.

"Chechi, it has been three months since I menstruated. I don't have a husband. I am in a desperate situation. I was in love with a final year P.G. student. I was to go home on revision leave the day before the exam, so I decided to spend some time in the evening with him on his insistence. I checked out from the hostel saying that I was going to the temple. He met me at the temple with another man whom he introduced as his relative.

We quickly returned from the temple and the three of us went to a hotel not too far away, and had coffee and vada. After a while I felt tired. I don't know what happened after that. When I was aware of my surroundings, we were standing on the road near a taxi.

"You fainted and had to rest for a while. Let's take a taxi to the hostel". They got inside the taxi and I followed them. I reached the hostel before eight o'clock and I did not go home the next day. I felt pain all over my body. However, I finished my written exams and my Practical exams too. I gave my college address to the University for my degree certificate to be posted. Then I travelled to this area and jumped into the lake to end my life."

Both Nivedita and Janu were quiet when they went down to have a cup of tea.

One day, two months later, Nivedita's mother saw Janu and asked her, "Are you pregnant, Janu?"

"Yes". she replied.

"Where is your husband?" was Mother's next question.

"I don't know." Janu clasped both her hands in distress.

"Why don't you know that?" asked amma.

"I really don't know, she replied unhappily.

On hearing that, mother got suspicious and left. Janu also went upstairs. At that moment, Achuthan came home and asked, "Amme, can I have a glass of tea?"

While drinking tea, Embranthiri asked mother, "Would you get Janu to marry me?" "Did you get only a whore to marry?" replied his mother in anger.

After a few days, Janu went to the college with chechi and collected her degree certificate and mark list. After showing them, she got a job as a teacher in a nearby school. While she was working, she started attending online P.G courses. When she started getting a salary, she began a 'Sharanalayam' for helpless women in the hall of their house, with the help of Nivedita chechi and her mother. Four other women joined her. After completing her M.A, she became a college lecturer.

Meanwhile, Achuthan approached Janu with a marriage proposal.

"I'm not interested in marrying anyone. I intend to focus on my job and Sharanalayam."

Achuthan walked away in despair.

On the last day of March, after the staff meeting, Janu reached home an hour early.

She looked closer to see elderly woman sitting back in a chair in the hall.

"Amme, where is my father?" I called my father several times a few days ago. No one picked up the phone."

Crying, mother said, "Bhanu's father passed away four months ago. There was no serious illness. Before he died, he asked for Bhanu to come home."

'Amme," Janu called out loudly, hugged her mother and cried. They sat there and wept for about fifteen minutes. Meanwhile, a little girl came there and asked "Why are you all crying?" and grabbed the hem of Janu's saree and pulled it. Janu said "nothing" to her and introduced the girl to her mother.

"Amme, she is my daughter, Lakshmi. She is five years old."

"Amme, how did you get in here, at the 'Sharanalayam'?" Bhanu asked her mother. Her mother replied, "When your father passed away, I had no one. I had some money at home. I took whatever possessions I had and began to search for you. I moved in and out of many buses."

Nivedita reached there by then. "She will tell you the rest later. Now let's have something to eat," she said and went inside the house with them.

Glossary

Amma/amme: Mother

Eatten: Elder brother

Chechi: Elder sister

Sharanalayam: A shelter for the needy and helpless women

10. The Oasis

Vilas More joined Class One at the end of June. He was happy. After a week, his happiness and anticipation plummeted. The boys in the class started hitting him and teasing him. His school phobia increased and he explained the bullying to his father, Jagtap More.

"After a few days your reluctance to go to school will change. You will have many friends to play with. So now, you go to school." After saying that, Jagtap More left for his workshop. Vilas also went to school reluctantly.

When Vilas arrived at school, all the children greeted him with smiles. When the bell rang for the interval, all the children gathered around him, making fun of him, pinching him and pushing him. When he cried, they all started laughing. He was silent and withdrawn. They started shouting that he had no mother and was an orphan, as he was in some way responsible for losing his mother. It was more than Vilas could bear. On hearing about it, his father said, "Don't worry, son" and hugged him. The next day, Vilas was sent to school with the housemaid. The children in the class mocked him saying that she was not his mother and she worked in many houses as a maid. Little children can be very cruel. Vilas went home and asked his father, "Thuja aai aahe kaa?" (Do I have a mother?) Jagtap More said to him."Mi tujhya aaila gheun yeina." (I will bring your mother.)

Vilas got promoted to the next class but the children did not leave him alone. As a result of the bullying, his confidence in himself dropped and he began to get low marks. The students in his class still made fun of him, teased and annoyed him saying, "The person living with you is not your father. He got Vilas from somewhere.

"Mii ashikshit aahe." (I am uneducated.) I cannot help you in your studies," his father told him.

Both of them exchanged their ideas in broken Marathi. One day Jagtap More said to Vilas, "Mi tujhya aaila gheun yein" (I will bring your mother.) Thu shant bus. Ek nahitar dono varsh." (May you be at peace for a year or two.) Tumala Cycle Sikonar. Tula changla vattel." (I will teach you to ride a bicycle. You will be happy.) When he started learning to ride a cycle, he began to feel more alert and enthusiastic.

Jagtap More showed Vilas an old photograph of a woman carrying a baby and said fondly, "See? Whose photo is this? This is a photo of you and your mother." "And where is my mother then? Why doesn't she come to see me?" Vilas enquired and cried non-stop. "Where does mother stay"

"Your mother and sister stay at her mother's house and live with her elder brother. Let's go there tomorrow," Jagtap said.

The next day both of them left to meet Vilas's mother. While they were talking to each other on the way, Vilas asked, "Why does mom live with uncle? Why can't she live with us?"

"I will tell you everything. Listen carefully." Jagtap began to say.

"One day, I came back from the workshop and did not find Pranali at home."

"Who is Pranali?" Vilas asked.

"Your mother." Jagtap replied.

"Then where did I go?" Vilas did not finish his sentence. Before that Jagtap said, "I didn't see you either. I searched many places but I didn't find you anywhere. You were only two years old. Finally, I went to your grandmother's house that night, looking for you. Both of you were there. I got very angry with her saying that she should not have gone there without telling me. I couldn't control myself.

"If you are coming, bring Vilas and come with me now," I told Pranali. She kept weeping and so I carried you home that night. Pranali didn't come with us. After that, we were the only ones left at home.

When they reached the courtyard of Pranali's mother's house, Jagtap strained his ears to listen for classical music by Bhimsen Joshi and ghazals by Pankaj Udhas. Both these Indian singers had always been Pranali's favourites. When he realized that he could not hear their haunting melodies, he was a little disappointed.

He shouted loudly, "Pranali, Pranali, come here and see who has come to see you." Pranali's younger sister, Aparna, took Vilas inside and asked Jagtap to sit down.

"Where is Pranali? Tell her to come here."

Aparna replied, "My sister is not here. She is in Muscat."

"You bring paper and pen and write her a letter for me. You know I don't know how to write."

He told Aparna what to write: "You should come home as soon as possible as Vilas is very sad. He is missing you very badly.

Yours,

Jagtap

As he was about to leave, Jagtap looked at Aparna and said, "After a few days, we are coming again to take Pranali."

Vilas was happy. After ten days, Jagtap More went there again with Vilas.

"Did Pranali come?" he asked. He was very nervous. There was silence for a while, then Pranali came out crying.

"On the day we parted, I was not even given a chance to tell you what had happened. My elder brother brought me a letter saying that my mother was sick and in a critical condition. The next afternoon, mother bade goodbye to us, and went to heaven." Pranali said.

"Don't remember that now. I made a mistake that day. I apologize. Let's hurry up and leave. Let's go." Saying that, Jagtap left for their home with Pranali and Vilas.

While Pranali was working in the kitchen, Vilas came behind her and said, "Tu kaya banavat aahe? (What are you making?) Aaj changla jeavan banava" (Make good food today.) He waited there. Pranali said she would make kuboos and worked hurriedly. Quoting the sheik, in whose house she had worked in Muscat, she told Jagtap that they could get a visa for Muscat in twelve days. The Sheik also said that he would find a job for Jagtap. Ten days later, Pranali received the envelope containing visas for the three of them. She was so overjoyed that she was dumbstruck. At last fortune was smiling on their lives

11. A Family Reunion and a Discourse on Love

"It has been a month since Aathira's call has come. She calls once every two weeks. I can't figure out why it's so late. Is it a network problem or something else? Isn't she in Canada?"

Kamala walked in and out of the room in a state of unease. She picked up her mobile phone and opened it.

"Ha! Here's Aathira's WhatsApp message." Kamala was happy. She read it eagerly. Aathira would be coming to Delhi in September, with her husband.

Mind blowing news! "It's been three years since I saw Aathira. This is the month of June. I can meet Aathira after three months. "

Kamala began to make plans in her mind. "If Aathira comes, we should take a trip somewhere for a week, with our families. She may not be able to stay many days in India. I have to convince her somehow. It's not good if we spend all our time at home. We need to visit some places."

With these thoughts, Kamala went to the kitchen and prepared dinner. By then, Vijayan had come from the office. While her husband was eating dinner, Kamala mentioned Aathira's plans to visit India in a few months.

"When they come, we can stay at a good resort for a week. We can also go sight-seeing. It should also be a place that will interest Nandumon. Isn't he a little boy?" Kamala vocalized her plans to Vijayan without much discussion.

"Let's think about it this weekend," Vijayan said and went to bed.

On Saturday, Kamala made rice flour appam and egg masala in the morning and called Vijayan for breakfast.

"I have made Vijayan and Nandumon's favourite dish today," Kamala said. The three of them laughed. After eating, they washed their hands and mouths and came back to the breakfast table. When Vijayan said, "Kamala, Nandumon should also participate in the discussion, shouldn't he?" Kamala replied, "He must, he must. We must know his opinion too."

Nandumon stared blankly for a moment and as understanding dawned on him, he said, "Aathira aunty and Dinesh uncle will be coming to Delhi from Canada in October. Mummy says we can all go somewhere and stay for a week with them. I feel we can go to

Jaipur or Udaipur and visit all the famous places of historical interest, particularly the Hawa Mahal, Amber Palace, the beautiful lakes, forts, temples, gardens and wildlife sanctuaries."

Vijayan opined, "It is not enough for us to decide like that. Shouldn't we take their wishes into account?"

"Yes, we should," Kamala and Nandu replied and left the discussion there.

The next night, Aathira called Kamala. She told her they had to take leave to come to India and reminded her again about their trip.

Then Kamala said, "It would be better if your arrival can be arranged by the end of October."

"Um...what's the matter?" asked Aathira.

"Nothing. If you come during Nandumon's vacation time, he will be happy. Also, during your stay here, we are thinking of a week-long getaway from Delhi to somewhere else for both our families. Vijayan will do the booking of the resort if you have no objection. Have your say."

"What if we flee to Kashmir? Aathira suggested. Dinesh supported the idea. "Okay. I'll talk about it with Vijayan. Then I'll send you a message."

"No. I'll call you within two weeks, Kamala." After saying this, Aathira disconnected the phone.

As planned, Athira and Dinesh came to Kamala's house in Delhi in the last week of October. Athira's parents were also there. They spent a week there happily. In the first week of November, Kamala, Vijayan, Nandumon, Athira and Dinesh travelled to Kashmir with their suitcases and bags. As the booking was done in advance, they got into the resort without any problems. Since it was one o'clock in the afternoon, they quickly ordered lunch and enjoyed the food. After resting for a while, Dinesh asked everyone, "Where do you want to go now? Tell me quickly." "I just want to see the lake." Nandu said. They took a car ride to see the lake in Kashmir. Anchored in Dal Lake, they saw many beautiful boats, decorated with flowers. When they came to know that they could book a stay in a 'floating house' or 'houseboat,' they made arrangements immediately to stay overnight. They slept in the houseboat after having a sumptuous meal on board. After the boat trip, they returned to the resort at 7 pm.

The next day, everyone got ready after the morning rituals and breakfast. Vijayan looked at the women and asked, "Where do you want to go today, ladies?"

Athira and Kamala said in unison, "Let's see all the gardens here."

Dinesh agreed saying, "Let it be so."

Kamala and Athira could not get enough of the beautiful blooms and scent of flowers as they went from one garden to the next.

While walking and enjoying the beauty of the plants and flowers, Athira asked Kamala, "Why did you cry on the previous day of your wedding and the next day during the muhurtha?" (auspicious time)

"I was in love with someone else. I couldn't forget my feelings so soon. You probably knew that." Kamala said.

"I knew that., but I didn't know how intense that love was?" Athira added.

By then Vijayan, Nandumon and Dinesh had joined them.

They returned to the resort by dusk. At night, Athira and Kamala shared a room, while Vijayan, Dinesh and Nandu slept in the next room. The lights were not turned off even though it was midnight. Dinesh, Vijayan and Nandu played chess, while Athira and Kamala shared their personal stories.

"I have never felt that it is a bad thing for a man or a woman to fall in love with someone he or she likes. Love is a sweet and private feeling. Sometimes people are in a state where their minds and emotions are in conflict. It may be that they have met many times, but they walk silently. When in love, one longs to see the loved one, but the affection may be in the mind or in the heart and one is happy just seeing each other. Sometimes you don't have to talk as you feel a deep sense of connection without having to communicate. Sometimes you want to talk about love and more," Kamala concluded.

"Can't you prepare a thesis on love?" Athira asked.

"You are mistaken. Love is not a word game. It will happen without warning. My office colleague, Madan Chaudhary and I fell in love. When I showed him my wedding invitation, he took it and blessed me.

"Thank you so much for the love you have given me all this time. May goodness always happen to you, Kamala, and may you always be well and happy," he said as tears fell from his eyes onto the invitation card.

Kamala stopped her reminiscences and Athira and Kamala fell asleep shortly after sharing this confidence.

The next morning, they all woke up very late. In the evening, they went to a studio and took pictures together to preserve their happy memories. Kamala and Athira posed as Kashmiri women and took separate photographs.

The next day, Kamala asked Athira about her love affair.

"It was only a passion for a very short period of time," Athira replied. "That is confidence for another day!"

Family Photos.

Late Husband
T.C,. Ramachandran

Publishing details

Contact us for publishing your own book.

Email I'D : aswanisomya1710@gmail.com

Contact no. : +91 8698468485